# The
# Friendship
# Fairies
## Go to Camp

# The Friendship Fairies Go to Camp

## LUCY KENNEDY

ILLUSTRATED BY
PHILLIP CULLEN

*Gill Books*

Gill Books
Hume Avenue
Park West
Dublin 12
www.gillbooks.ie

Gill Books is an imprint of M.H. Gill and Co.

Text © Lucy Kennedy 2021
Illustrations © Phillip Cullen 2021

978 07171 8966 3

Edited by Sheila Armstrong
Copy-edited by Jane Rogers
Proofread by Jennifer Armstrong
Printed by BZ Graf S.A., Poland

This book is typeset in 14 on 28pt, Baskerville.
The paper used in this book comes from the wood pulp
of managed forests. For every tree felled, at least one
tree is planted, thereby renewing natural resources.

A CIP catalogue record for this book is available from
the British Library.

5 4 3 2 1

# CONTENTS

To all of my young readers.
Whenever you are feeling sad, know
that a fairy is looking after you.

# CHAPTER ONE
## Poor Farmer George

'Run! **RUN**, you slowcoach!' yelled Holly at the top of her voice, her big brown eyes wild and her long shiny hair all over her face.

'I'm trying!' shouted Jess. Her legs were shorter than her older sister's, but they could really move when she was under pressure. Why, oh why, had Holly got them into this mess?

They jumped over the fence like champion racehorses, landing on their bottoms … right in a huge, dirty puddle.

'Holy moly, my butt is like ice now!' panted Holly. 'Come on, Jess.' She reached out her hand and pulled Jess up and out of the water. Off they ran, soaking wet and giggling, Holly's Airy-Fairy Converse runners making squelching noises.

When they got closer to their neighbourhood, the sisters flicked out their wings and jumped into the air. They flew up their tree and over to their treehouse, adding a few cheeky somersaults and backflips as they went.

As they approached their front door, they could see their mother standing there, looking very cross and with her arms folded. Their mum was usually very chilled, so this meant *big* trouble. Oh dear.

'I'll do the talking,' whispered Holly to Jess, who looked worried. 'I know how to play this lady.'

'*This lady* can hear you, Holly. You seem to forget that I *also* have magical powers!' said Mrs Dixon, pointing inside the treehouse. 'Inside, please.'

She ushered them in quickly because Mr and Mr Snail were nearby, eavesdropping as usual. They were known for being right old gossips!

The girls flew into their house, avoiding their mum's annoyed gaze. They had a feeling that they were in serious trouble this time. Their big sister, Emme, was in the Enchanted Mall with her friends, so she was not even around to defend them.

'So,' began Mrs Dixon, 'I believe that you two were annoying Farmer George in the village. *Again*?' She was pacing now, with her hands crossed behind her back. 'Not looking good,' thought Holly, trying to look sad and cute at the same time. This face sometimes worked wonders.

'Stealing his baby carrots and using him as a human **dartboard**,' said Mrs Dixon, 'while the poor old man was minding his own business and sunbathing in his garden?'

Jess giggled. She had catapulted her carrot right into his big red nose. He had got such a fright, jumping up and screaming like a banshee!

'Jessica Dixon!' her mum snapped. 'I can assure you that nothing about this is funny, at all. First of all, you are not allowed onto farms because you are so small and, second, he *saw* you! A human saw you both. You broke the **fairy-safe code**! Now Farmer George will be very confused, and his poor nose will be throbbing.'

'Gemma, it was Harry's idea,' blurted out Holly, determined to defend herself and her sister to the end. She always used her mum's first name when she was trying to win an argument. Harry lived next door to them, with his brothers, Ollie and Hugo.

'That's *Mum* to you, thank you, Holly, and I'm not concerned about Harry,' said Mrs Dixon. 'His parents are next door talking to him right now, and they are *just* as annoyed as I am.'

Jess aimed her pointed ear at the wall to see if she could hear her next-door neighbours. She didn't hear anything. But this might have been because Mr Barns had a very quiet voice. He worked in the town library, so he spent his life whispering. Sometimes he whispered so quietly, even outside work, that people couldn't hear him.

'So, in light of this behaviour,' Mrs Dixon said, 'we have decided that you are going to **Camp Tír na nÓg** for four weeks. Maybe there you will learn the importance of responsibility!'

'But ... but ... I don't speak Irish well enough,' Holly stammered. Irish was not her strongest subject, and Tír na nÓg was an Irish-speaking camp. 'Actually, I don't speak it at all, now that I think about it ... I mean, I know dog is *madra*, but that's it!' she said, panicked all of a sudden.

'You'll get by, Holly,' her mum said. 'They speak English there too. Emme is going as well, to keep an eye on you two! And I've spoken to Betty and Charles Barns next door and they agree that their triplets will be going too. Maybe then you'll learn how to behave!'

Holly and Jess looked at each other, worried, but knowing better than to argue when their mum was in this mood.

The sisters quickly had showers to warm up after the dip in the puddle, then got into their fluffy pyjamas. Holly spent some time cleaning mud off her turquoise Converse – they were her favourite shoes.

Downstairs, Mrs Dixon was talking to Emme as she served up magic beans on homemade bread. Emme was not happy with her sisters. She had planned to go to the mall and hang out with her friends over the summer, not get dirty in a caravan park with her irresponsible sisters and annoying boy neighbours! Holly and Jess walked into the kitchen, looking guilty, and Emme gave them a dirty look.

The three little fairies ate in silence and then went straight to bed, tired and slightly worried. Holly was thinking of all the Irish words she knew. There weren't very many. How would she manage in an Irish-speaking camp?

The girls tossed and turned for a while and had trouble falling asleep. When Jess heard their parents talking quietly downstairs, she slipped out of bed and gently cracked the door open so that all three of them could listen.

'I honestly think that it will be the making of them, Gemma,' Mr Dixon was saying. 'There will be amazing volunteers to supervise them, and the girls will learn more of their national language. What could possibly go wrong? I think the girls will have a great adventure.'

'An **adventure**?' Holly sat up in bed. 'Yeah, baby, now we're talking.'

'An adventure!' her sisters replied at the same time, and they all burst out laughing in their bunk beds. A summer adventure with the Barns brothers in Tír na nÓg. That sounded like fun, didn't it?

# CHAPTER TWO
## Sir Prize's Castle

On Saturday morning, the Dixon sisters got up and had some fly-fly cereal, which was shaped like butterflies, and then waited for their parents to come downstairs. They were half excited and half nervous. They had never been to a camp before, so they had no idea what to expect – they didn't even know where the camp was!

They had spent the night before drinking hot fairberry juice and packing their clothes into their backpacks. Holly had started packing six suitcases, one filled entirely with scrunchies, but her parents told her that she was only allowed one backpack. They could share their stuff with each other at camp.

'Morning, girls,' Mrs Dixon said, coming down the stairs. 'We're going to go to **Sir Prize's castle** now, and Betty, Charles and the boys will meet us there.'

Holly's tummy did a little flip with excitement. She loved spending time with her best friend, Harry.

'Why are we going there, Mum?' asked Emme, who always needed to know exactly what was going on. As the eldest, she felt responsible for her two younger sisters.

'You'll see,' said their dad, helping them put on their coats. They had a few bags between them, so he had ordered a Butterfly Taxi, who was waiting patiently outside their front door. The Dixon family got on, put on their seatbelts, and the butterfly gracefully took off.

A few minutes into the journey, Mrs Dixon turned around to the girls. 'Now listen up, you three. You are going to have a great time at the camp. The people working there will look after you. But you will need to **behave**!'

Holly and Jess looked at each other guiltily. Emme sighed. She would have her hands full keeping those two in line.

'If you need to, girls, you can contact us using this,' Mrs Dixon said, handing Emme a pink glittery pen with a unicorn head that bobbed and shone. 'This is Uni. He has been in our family since my great great granny was your age, and he's never, *ever* let any of us down.'

'How does he work?' asked Holly. She was shocked that she hadn't discovered this magical pen during one of her secret rooting sessions.

She was an expert at snooping.

'He'll show you how when the time comes,' said Gemma. 'But only use him when you *really* need him, okay?'

Emme nodded and packed Uni into the front of her backpack, making a mental note not to let Holly near him, ever.

The rest of the journey was spent admiring the view. The Butterfly Taxis could fly higher than the fairies, right below the clouds, so they got to see life below them in a new light.

Arriving at Sir Prize's castle created great excitement in the taxi. Jess gave a whoop of joy. 'We're here!' she said. 'Should we get out?' she asked her parents.

'Yes, please,' her dad said, as he petted the butterfly to say thank you.

They could see a small group at the front door – a man, a woman and three nervous-looking boys. As they got closer, they could see it was the Barns family.

'Hello, everyone,' said Betty Barns, turning round. She was looking very fancy today in her best outfit, with a hairband made of fresh daisies, and a bright orange coat.

The two fathers shook hands. 'Hello,' said Mr Barns, in his librarian voice. He was a very tall man, with red glasses that matched his hair.

The massive front door opened, and a well-dressed mookie invited them in. It had a round face shaped like a cookie, with a wiggly nose and ears like a mouse. The mookies helped Sir Prize take care of his castle.

'My boss is waiting for you all in the drawing room,' it said.

The group walked into the castle together, looking around in awe. It was **huge**!

'Harry, what are we doing here?' asked Holly when she caught up with her partner in crime.

'I'm not sure, to be honest, Hols,' said Harry, looking uneasy. 'Maybe Sir Prize gives us a map to the camp or something. Would you like me to carry your luggage for you?' Harry wanted to show her how strong he was becoming.

'No, thank you, Harry, and welcome to the 21st century,' said Holly. 'It's great to have you here.' She took great pride in her independence and hated being offered help. Even so, she struggled to get up the stairs with her heavy backpack, and left a trail of scrunchies behind her!

The grand drawing room was full of silver trinkets and comfy couches. 'Hello,' said Sir Prize, who was standing beside the blazing fire with his hands behind his back. 'I'm so glad that you've decided to help me.'

The six youngsters looked at each other, completely confused, but then smiled politely. How were they expected to help Sir Prize when they were supposed to be going to a camp?

'Let me bring you upstairs,' Sir Prize said, 'and I hope that you all enjoy yourselves.'

They all walked up the stairs and over to a big silver door that was covered with locks and cameras that followed their every move. 'The secret door,' Emme thought. She had first seen this mysterious door last year at a party in the castle. What was going on here?

Sir Prize took out a huge ring of keys and began to unlock the door, which took some time. 'We keep it locked up tight to make sure nothing magical sneaks out into the human world. The **fairy-safe code** always comes first – keeping magical creatures safe from humans *and* protecting humans from magic.'

Holly and Jess tried not to look at each other. Poor Farmer George and his big red nose!

'Welcome,' said Sir Prize, as the huge door creaked open, 'to **Tír na nÓg**!'

Through the doorway, the group could see a forest, with people and animals walking around. There was a circle of white caravans, a huge campfire, and, through a gap in the trees, they could just about see the blue of the ocean.

Sir Prize smiled at the six confused young faces. 'I set up a special camp on this magical island three hundred years ago,' he said. 'It's an incredibly special place, where you can learn our beautiful language while helping our animals and the planet.'

'Goodbye, girls, and remember – use Uni if you *really* need us,' said Mr and Mrs Dixon.

The Barns family were hugging each other at the same time. Mr Barns was whispering, 'Have a ball, and behave yourselves, please, boys. Don't be annoying anyone, now!'

'We will,' they all shouted in unison, adjusting their backpacks, and heading down the path and into the bright green busy forest.

'*Fáilte romhat!* Welcome!' said a smiley, friendly girl walking towards them. '*Is mise*

Sinead, and I'll be your camp coach.' Emme thought she looked very cool, with her purple hair, piercings and trendy clothes. She decided that as soon as she was old enough, she was going to get her nose pierced!

'Let me show you guys around,' said Sinead, walking towards some caravans. There were people sitting on logs around the huge campfire at the centre of the camp, and others were leading different animals through the forest.

Holly had never seen some of the animals before. 'Wow!' she thought. 'This is going to be possibly *the* most exciting thing that has *ever* happened to me.' Although she was only young, Holly felt like she had lived a lifetime.

'You are staying in Caravan Seven, girls,' Sinead said, standing outside a grubby-looking trailer. She turned to the Barns brothers. 'And you, *mo chairde*, are opposite them, in Caravan Eight.'

'Okay,' the two groups said, opening their caravan doors.

# CHAPTER THREE
## Camp Tír na nÓg

'Ah here, you must be joking, mate!' shrieked Holly, as she walked into the caravan, her face turning pale. She dropped her backpack and pretended to faint.

The caravan was very dark, very drab and very bare. It had three single beds, a stove and a table with three chairs.

Holly's eyes drifted towards a door which had *Leithreas* written on it. Inside, there was a tiny little bathroom with a shower, a smelly loo and a sink with a bar of soap.

'**Nooo!**' she shouted at her sisters, who were trying to hold back their smiles. 'Are we meant to do our business in *that*?!'

She looked so annoyed and disgusted that Emme and Jess burst out laughing. Holly was big into cleanliness and carried hand gel everywhere with her. She spent her life cleaning anything and everything she came across, so this was her idea of a nightmare.

'It's okay, Hols,' said Jess, who was just relieved to see that they had soap. 'We can make it homely, and it's only for four weeks.'

'Emme, get the magic unicorn pen thing out – maybe it can clean the room and paint it pink,' said Holly, working up a sweat as she paced the caravan.

'No, Holly. Now cop on,' Emme said calmly in her older-sister voice. 'This is fine. We are not going to waste Uni's time on this.'

So the little fairies unpacked their .

belongings (Holly dramatically holding her nose) and put their teddies on their beds.

'Not a great start,' thought Holly, who was keeping an eye on the door of Caravan Eight. She could hear Elf Rock playing through the window and she wanted to see if the Barns' caravan was as manky as theirs!

When they were settled in, Sinead knocked on the door. 'Okay, my friends,' she said cheerily. 'Let's go and meet everyone else.'

The girls' mouths fell open as Sinead led them deeper into the camp. There were lots of mookies pushing wheelbarrows around, and some Piggy-flies flying above them, playing chase. They were a funny pairing, because the mookies were very gentle and serious and the Piggy-flies were zooming around, trying to annoy them!

There were lots of other campers too. Some were in hiking clothes, but most were wearing trackies and wellies. There was even one guy in a scuba suit.

Sinead talked them through everything. 'This is the **Camp Circle**,' she said, pointing to where most of the activity was going on. It was a ring of wooden benches surrounding a bonfire in a large clearing. Some people were wearing red T-shirts that said *Is mise TÍR NA nÓG.*

'The people wearing red T-shirts are staff members,' said Sinead as she saw Jess staring at them. 'If you have a problem, anything at all, these are safe people that you can talk to. Also, Sir Prize has security all over the camp to protect us all.'

The sisters nodded. Emme knew it was important to talk to a friend or an adult you can rely on if you are worried, or if something

does not feel right in your heart. She took this very seriously because she was the eldest sister.

'Over here is the food station,' said Sinead, pointing.

Jess followed Sinead's finger and saw a massive straw hut with picnic tables underneath, swarming with people. The tables had different flags as tablecloths, and music was blaring from speakers set into the straw thatch roof.

'*An bhfuil ocras ort*? Are you hungry?' she smiled kindly.

'Yes!' said Jess. 'Let's do this,' she added, rubbing her little hands together and skipping over to the hut. The smell of the food had been wafting right up her curious little nostrils. If she was not talking about food, she was thinking about it!

They all laughed and followed Jess. Behind the counter was an incredibly large chef. He was very tall, and very, very, very wide, and he was singing at the top of his voice. He had messy brown hair that he kept pushing off his face and into his huge hairnet.

The closer they got, the more they realised that, nice as he looked, this chef could *not* sing. He was belting out 'Baby Shark' in a funny Italian accent and using two wooden spoons to act out the moves. Completely bonkers!

'Charlie. Charlie! **CHARLIE**!' yelled Sinead, pretty much in his face. 'Let me introduce you to our new campers.'

'Ah, c'mere, *céad míle fáilte!*' he said, putting down his wooden spoons and flipping the sausages (or at least they looked like sausages).

'*Ciao*,' said Holly. 'Lovely singing,' she added quietly.

'Holly!' said Emme. They were in an Irish camp – surely Holly could at least try to speak a few words of it? '*Is mise* Emme, and this is Holly and Jess,' she said, introducing her younger sisters.

'Girls, you're welcome, *fáilte*, you're welcome,' said Charlie, smiling. 'Now, what's on the menu today …' he said, like he was presenting a TV talent show. Emme looked behind her, expecting to see cameras and a stage.

'Mushroom twisty-wisty pasta, with creamy frog saucy-sauce. The crusty bread was freshly made this morning in the Gnome Bakery, and for dessert I have my secret ice cream with a dripping toffee-apple sauce.'

'Phew,' thought Emme. The caravans

weren't great, but at least the food looked nice!

'*A chara*, enjoy your *béile* and I'll see you in a bit,' said Sinead, running off towards the other camp leaders.

The sisters sat down together to eat lunch. Holly was delighted to see Harry and his brothers come into the food station with their camp leader. The boys got their food and looked around. When Harry saw Holly waving at him, he grinned and told his brothers to follow him over to the girls.

'Ah, Holly!' said Emme. She really did not like the Barns boys, and she didn't want to get stuck with them for the summer. 'Why did you have to ask them over to our table?'

'Emme,' said Holly through her smile, 'Please #bekind. The **fairy-safe code** says to be kind to everyone, remember?'

'How are you getting on, Hols?' said Harry.

'Ah grand, neighbourino,' said Holly, and they chatted away easily, comparing their caravans. Holly was happy to hear that Caravan Eight was just as yucky as theirs.

When they had finished eating, they copied the other campers and brought their plates over to the Scrape and Bin stand around the back. A sign said that all the food was divided and reused, either on the land or to feed the magical creatures.

A few minutes later, a whistle was blown.
It was a strange whistle that sounded quite like
a short version of *Riverdance*. Jess expected the
leaders to start Irish dancing, but it didn't happen
– she was a bit disappointed! Irish dancing is very
important to fairies because they believe that it
creates positive energy in the world.

'*Bailígí thart* – gather around, everyone,' shouted Sinead, standing beside a red-headed girl whose name badge said Michelle. People came out of the trees and caravans and gathered around the Camp Circle. There were around forty people in total.

'Okay,' Sinead said. 'We'll split you up into three different groups. First, we have *An Fharraige* – the Ocean Zone. Next is *Ainmhithe* – the Animal Zone. And finally, *Na Coille* – the Forest Zone. If you can all queue up in front of Michelle, we will give you each a coloured piece of paper.'

'*Ainmhithe* – yes please!' said Holly, who loved animals. She winked at Harry, who was looking a bit nervous. He loved animals too and wanted to be a vet. More important, he wasn't an ocean person – he was allergic to lobsters!

# CHAPTER FOUR
## New Jobs

Sure enough, Harry, Holly and Jess were soon heading over to the Animal Zone gate. Emme, Ollie and Hugo decided to go to the Ocean Zone.

At the Animal Zone gate, there was a young guy with a clipboard talking to the group that had already formed. There were about ten other campers of all shapes and sizes, each one looking nervous and excited.

'*Is mise* Fionn, and I'm the Animal Zone leader,' he said. 'Trust me – you are going to want to wear wellies!' He pointed to a huge pile of boots in every size you could imagine.

Holly was delighted that they were wearing the camp wellies – she would absolutely freak out if she got even a speck on her sparkly turquoise Converse again. She loved them so much, in fact, that she raced back to her caravan to tuck them under her pillow!

'Now,' said Fionn, 'at Tír na nÓg we have Piggy-flies, Chunga-Wungas, Lady-braiders,

Nip-gits, Furry-baz and, of course, unicorns. They all need to be fed, cleaned and cared for. Some are friendly, and some may nibble, so keep your hands to yourself if you see a sign that says "I BITE"!' he laughed.

Fionn led them down a dirty, mucky path into a clearing, the mud squishing under their wellies. All around, there were lots of huge pens and enclosures. There were plenty of noises coming from the animals, some very high pitched and some lower, like growling and banging.

'Okay,' Fionn said, 'have a look around and see which animal you feel that you can work with. Some of these animals have sad stories, some have happy stories. A few of them were rescued from families who did not want them any more and a few of them came here because they were injured and unable to look after themselves.'

Holly, Harry and Jess stuck together as they walked around the zone, up and down the paths. There were no cages or glass windows, which made Harry happy. All the animals had big open pens and comfortable beds.

'A Chunga-Wunga? What's that?' asked Holly, looking into a big pen. She read a sign beside the pen: 'A Chunga-Wunga is like a chubby chimpanzee who doesn't know when to stop eating – ever. They have huge, pointed ears, a front pocket like a kangaroo, and they can turn invisible when they are nervous. They are usually pink with purple stripes and like to have their hair brushed.'

'I think I've just met my soulmate,' Holly squealed, making the others jump. She was **obsessed** with brushing hair – anyone's hair – and if she could French plait it, even better!

Jess thought to herself, 'That poor Chunga-Wunga has no idea what she's getting into!'

Just then, a beautiful animal with silky fur
came out of the hut. Her eyes were dark brown,
and she was wearing a hairband. But when she
saw them looking, she immediately disappeared!
All that was left was the hairband and a pink
wiggly nose.

'Ah, I see you've met Riley the Chunga-Wunga,' Fionn said, walking over to the threesome. 'Yes, she is very special indeed. Somebody had her as a pet, but as soon as the owner realised that an animal involves time and commitment, she was left outside in a cold shed to fend for herself. That's when Sir Prize rescued her. He can't stand animal cruelty.'

'That's so sad,' Harry said.

'But remember, campers, Riley is one of the lucky ones – because she's here, with you!' Fionn continued. 'If you want her to show herself, what you need to do is **earn her trust**. Only then will she let you brush her hair.'

So Holly sat with Riley the Chunga-Wunga for the next few hours and tried to talk and sing to her. Most of Riley's body stayed invisible but, very slowly, her ears started to reappear. She was curious about all the funny-looking people around her, but she was very unsure of them. Especially the loud brown-haired girl who kept winking at her!

In an enclosure next door, Harry was looking after two magical hens. They were twins called Harriet and Sheila. They literally never stopped talking to each other and often they would both talk at the same time!

After a few hours, and a del

lunch from the Gnome Bakery, ]

and said it was time to finish up

'I'll see you tomorrow, Riley,' h

and all the campers headed back for dinner.

Emme, Ollie and Hugo were full of stories from the Ocean Zone. They had gone out in a boat with a glass floor to look at the bottom of the ocean. They saw lots of interesting sea creatures, but also saw how dirty the ocean was.

'We're actually getting into the water tomorrow,' Ollie said. 'We have so much rubbish and plastic to pick up, it's unbelievable.'

Emme looked over and smiled at him. She had always seen him as an annoying neighbour, but now she was starting to think that he might be growing into a nice, considerate person.

The six of them finished their food and walked back to the caravans.

'*Oíche mhaith!*' said Sinead as she passed by.

'Goodnight,' the Dixon girls said, trying not to yawn too obviously, because their parents said that it was rude.

Once in the caravan, they changed into their pyjamas in silence, brushed their teeth and got straight into bed. Five minutes later, they were fast asleep (after Holly had kissed her Converse goodnight).

# CHAPTER FIVE
## The Ocean

The following morning, the girls were woken by the sound of a loud noise coming from the Camp Circle. Jess opened the door and saw that it was one of the camp Furry-baz. They looked like small yellow teddy bears and they could make a noise that sounded like an air horn.

'Don't even think about it, mister!' Holly was saying, still fast asleep. She was obviously having an argument with someone in her dream. 'Oh yeah?' she shouted, eyes still closed. 'Well, if you so much as *touch* them, I'll turn you into a **furry caterpillar**!'

Jess looked at Emme and they tried not to laugh. 'Her new Converse,' they said at the same time, getting out of bed. 'Holly, wake up and stop being weird,' said Jess.

Holly shot up, her hair all over the place. 'Morning,' she said, with no memory of the fight from her dream.

The girls dressed more practically in jumpsuits today. Holly and Jess were going to be working in the Animal Zone again with Harry, while Emme was going to be cleaning the ocean.

Wellies on, they headed towards the Camp Circle. They could already see it was a hive of activity, buzzing with people, some eating breakfast, some chatting.

'Ah, the Dixons,' said Michelle, who looked very cool in her red T-shirt. 'Good morning. I hope you all slept okay. Your parents phoned me last night to check how you were all getting on, and I told them everything was grand so far. Now, get some *bricfeasta*, and then join your groups.'

Chef Charlie was singing again, but at least it was a bit quieter this time. They filled their plates with smoky red velvet pancakes covered with trickling honey sauce, and found a big table. The Barns triplets joined them a few minutes later.

'I'm so excited to see the ocean and what's in it,' said Ollie enthusiastically.

'Me too,' Emme said. She was hoping that she could really make a difference on this project.

'Ocean Zone, over here, please,' said Oisín, their team leader.

Emme hugged her sisters, wished them good luck, and then headed over with Ollie and Hugo.

There were maybe eight others in total. There were twins called Isobel and Daniella (known to everyone as Ibby and Dibby), who spoke no English whatsoever, but who spoke brilliant Irish. There were three loud goblin boys, who all wore matching stripy pyjama outfits. Then there were a couple of fairies with bright red hair and green eyes. And finally, there was a tiny blonde elf on her own.

'Nice group,' Emme thought, catching the elf's eye.

'I'm Kate,' said the elf. 'I'm here on my own. I have no brothers and sisters, so my parents thought that this would be a nice way to make new friends. I'm really looking forward to the Ocean Zone, are you?'

'I'm Emme,' Emme said, smiling. 'I'm here with my two *crazy* sisters. Yes, I'm excited, but I'm also a bit nervous that we'll find yucky things!'

'Let's go,' said Oisín, leading the group down a very muddy path. After about ten minutes, the path started changing from mud to sand. Emme could hear the waves. Yesterday, they had gone out in a boat, but today, they would actually be getting into the water.

Around a bend, the path widened and in front of them was the most beautiful stretch of beach. The sea looked so sparkly and clear and the sand was almost white.

'It looks beautiful,' said Oisín, 'but when you really look, you'll be shocked at what lies beneath the surface.'

He walked down to the water's edge and picked up the sea in his right hand, as if it was a duvet. Under the water, on the seabed, they could see old furniture, bags, rubbish, bottles,

tins and plastic. Ibby and Dibby groaned loudly
and wrinkled their noses.

'This is why we are here,' continued Oisín
gently, as he dropped the ocean down again.
'There is life in there among all of that human
rubbish, so our job is to clean up the mess. We
owe it to **our environment and our
ocean friends**.'

The team made a base in a sand dune near a hut and dropped their bags. Oisín opened the hut door and started handing out gear for the day. Everyone got a shovel, bag, gloves, wetsuit and pick-up stick.

They all wiggled and giggled their way into their wetsuits and then the snorkels were handed out. The red-haired fairies had some trouble getting all their hair to fit under their swimming hats. Anyone who wasn't a strong swimmer got armbands to help them float. The goblin boys put on two pairs each!

'I hope that the water's warm,' laughed Emme to her new friend Kate. She was trying not to think about having to use the loo. This always happened to her when she was near water!

'Me too,' said Kate. 'It looks okay so far …'

'Just to let you know, guys,' Oisín said, 'there are toilets at the back of the hut.'

'He just read my mind,' thought Emme, surprised. These team leaders were very cool indeed. Maybe that was why they were handpicked by Sir Prize himself. 'Maybe,' she thought, 'I might even be picked to be a camp leader someday.'

Ollie, Hugo, Emme and Kate made their way to the water's edge to join the other swimmers.

'Stay close to each other,' said Oisín, 'We swim as a group. Don't go into water deeper than you can stand up in. Pick up what you can and bring it back to the shore.'

They all slowly waded into the water. Emme held her breath a bit – the water was cold but not freezing. She put on her snorkel and followed Ollie as he dived into the sea.

Once her ears were under the water, she warmed up, and a lovely calm feeling washed over her. She couldn't hear a thing, except her own thoughts and slow breathing.

Within seconds, she began to see that the seabed was covered in plastic cups, bottles and tins. A lot of the plastic was wrapped around what she thought were rocks. She bent down to start picking it all up when something moved beneath her. '**Aaagghh**!' She tried to shout, but only a stream of bubbles came out. She quickly popped up to the surface.

'What's wrong, Emme?' Oisín asked, appearing beside her.

'Something moved!' Emme said in a panic, her snorkel hanging off and her heart beating fast.

'It's okay, Emme. Sorry, I forgot to warn you. They are sea-green turtles,' said Oisín, 'and sadly, they are trapped in all the plastic. They're friendly and won't hurt you – they are just stuck. Be gentle and try to free them.'

Emme laughed at her own fright and put her snorkel back on. She swam back over to start removing the plastic from the turtles. Oisín was right – they were very gentle. They also seemed grateful for the help and when they were freed, they swam around Emme as if to say thank you.

The team worked for a few hours. They stopped at lunchtime for a prepared Gnome Bakery picnic, which they ate on the sand as the sun shone above them.

'How lucky am I?' thought Emme, as she sat on the warm sandy beach, eating a jammy-whammy roll, her new friend Kate beside her and the beautiful ocean in front of her.

After their day at the seaside, they headed back to camp, had hot showers, dressed and walked over to meet the others at the Camp Circle.

At every bench, campers were telling stories about their day, and the atmosphere was electric. Holly was telling everyone that Riley the Chunga-Wunga had shown a bit of her knees today. She was convinced that they were 'bonding'.

After a dinner of spaghetti-fraschetti in a creamy sauce, they all headed back to their caravans.

'Night, you two, love you,' said Emme, exhausted after her long day's work.

Holly didn't reply, and soon her snores could be heard throughout the camp.

# CHAPTER SIX
## Jess and the Treeps

After the first week, they were all given the opportunity to move to a new zone or stay where they were. The camp leaders wanted every camper to follow their hearts, because if they cared about where they were working, they wouldn't complain!

Emme had chosen to stay working with the ocean team and Holly and Harry had chosen the animals. But Jess was intrigued about the

Forest Zone, so she asked Hugo Barns to join her.

They waved goodbye to the others and went over to Jack, who was the Forest Zone leader.

Jess looked down at her backpack and squeezed Uni. Emme had insisted that she brought him 'just in case'.

They walked down the path into what looked like a massive rainforest. The trees were so tall that they almost blocked out the sky. There were strange noises coming from the trees, almost like voices whispering. They could see something moving but couldn't make out what was in there.

'Say hello to the Treeps,' said Jack.

'What are Treeps?' asked Hugo, puzzled.

79

'Treeps are magic people who live in the forest. They live on the branches in handmade huts and **they protect and feed the trees**.'

Jess waved into the darkness, and saw the shapes of small people waving back at her. 'Why have I never seen any Treeps before?' she asked.

'They are very private,' Jack explained. 'They don't want to come down to us because they are happiest when they are in the trees. They are worried that trees are being cut down all over the world, because they understand how important trees are.'

They wandered on, deep into the forest. Jess could see gaps in the distance, where trees had been cut down. They looked terrible.

'That's why they are protecting this place,' Jack said. 'Before Sir Prize set up this camp, the forest was being destroyed. But he cleared out the tree-cutters and started to replant what they had cut down. Then he moved in the Treeps, who said that they would protect his land and the trees.'

In a clearing in the centre of the forest, the group had their sandwiches from the Gnome

Bakery. Afterwards, they were encouraged to climb the trees if they liked.

'The Treeps will look after you while you're up there,' Jack said. 'But make sure you are very gentle – the Treeps get very angry if you hurt one of the trees.'

Jess, of course, decided to climb the tallest tree that she could find. It was very old and very twisty, but its leaves were still bright green.

Hugo offered to help her, but she insisted that she wanted to climb it alone. So instead, he climbed up the tree beside hers, humming to himself.

As Jess climbed up her huge tree, she passed a smiling Treep, who waved at her, and she continued going up and up. As she climbed each branch, it got quieter and quieter and before she knew it, she'd climbed the whole way to the top.

When she stood up, her head poked up above all the other trees – she was actually in the clouds!

'Oh dear,' she thought. It was one thing getting up a tree – but how would she get down? Jess thought about flying down, but she'd never been this high up before and she was too scared. She looked down to see if Hugo was nearby, but all she could see was darkness. Above her head, the wind was getting stronger, making the tree sway over and back.

She could feel her legs starting to shake, and she knew that she had gone too far. What was she going to do?

Something in her backpack nudged her. It was Uni, the magic pen, reminding her that it was there. She pulled it out of her bag. 'Help me, please,' she begged.

Within seconds, a bubbly cloud popped out of the top of the pen and her parents appeared!

'Are you okay, love?' asked her mum.

'I climbed too high and now I'm stuck in a tree,' said Jess, relieved to hear the familiar voices.

'Okay, Jess, is there a Treep around?' her dad
asked. Jess was too distracted to even think about

asking him how he knew about Treeps! 'Hold Uni out, and I'll see if there is one nearby,' he added.

Jess held Uni below her, back under the treetops, keeping her eyes closed so as not to see the long fall below her.

Suddenly, she could hear her dad talking – but he was speaking a completely different language. It sounded like a mixture of buzzing noises and rustling leaves.

The branches below started to shake a little and when she opened her eyes, she saw a smiling Treep heading up towards her. Mr Dixon said something and the Treep gently took Jess's hand.

Up close, the Treep looked like a fairy, but her skin was green, and her hair was rough, like tree bark. Jess felt very relaxed in her presence, almost sleepy.

'Hold her hand and close your eyes, Jess,' her dad said calmly. 'This is Emilette, and she'll look after you.'

Jess did as she was told and when she felt the Treep let go of her hand, she opened her eyes. She was standing safely on the ground, still gripping Uni in the other hand. 'How?' she thought, looking up. Emilette waved down at her as she climbed back up into the tree.

'Oh hi, Jess,' said Hugo, jumping off the lowest branch of his tree. He'd missed all the drama. 'Are you ready to head back to camp?'

'I'm *never* leaving the ground again!' thought Jess, putting Uni safely back into her backpack.

# CHAPTER SEVEN
## Reaching Riley

In the meantime, there was so much happening in the Animal Zone.

The Guinea-bees were flying in swarms high above the pens. Harriet and Sheila, the hens, were watching Holly and whispering to each other, as if they were spying. Holly was convinced that all the animals gathered around the hen sisters every night for a tea party and a good ol' gossip about the campers!

Harry was busy working with some beautiful unicorns who were recovering from surgery in the Uni-Clinic. They were such beautiful and gentle creatures. They had a lovely calm way about them, and they would bow their heads in respect if someone helped them.

They had arrived at the camp in a terrible state a few months ago and were only now beginning to trust people enough to let them touch them. The poor unicorns had lived in cities, on grass fields surrounded by houses. People rode them on rough roads and did not get them the right care. While they were in the human world, they kept their magic horns invisible. It is only when a unicorn is happy and feeling safe that the horn appears.

It was very hard work looking after them all. The campers never stopped, except to break for lunch. Their backs were sore, and their hands were cut and red. Holly's hair was looking matted from the wind – and usually she didn't like to have a single hair out of place.

'Holy moly,' she said one day, breathing out loudly through the nose peg that she put on when she was cleaning poo. 'Animals are serious work, aren't they? Not just cute faces to pet!'

Harry looked up and smiled at his friend. 'They need us, Hols,' he said, bending down to clean a unicorn's hoof. Stella the unicorn had been limping badly, but she was on the mend. 'They can't talk, so if we can't help them, they'll suffer, like Stella here.' He patted her on the nose.

'I think I might be getting somewhere with Riley, you know,' said Holly proudly. The day before, Riley had come out of her house and walked straight over towards Holly. She sat in front of her with her back turned, but she had stayed visible the whole time. She had even let Holly brush her hair for a short time.

Harry had watched as Holly worked her
magic, being kind and patient, telling Riley
every single knock-knock joke that she knew.

'Riley, you and I are destined to be friends,'
she had said, and Riley looked right around at
her ... and **SPAT** in her hair!

'That is very rude, Riley,' said Holly very, very crossly, 'and I don't know if you are trying to be cool or not, but I would rather you didn't spit at me.'

With that, Riley had burst out laughing,
holding her chest and rolling around on the
ground. Holly was shocked. She had never
heard an animal laugh, let alone a Chunga-
Wunga. It sounded like a car starting!

So Holly jumped up, furious and red-faced, looking Riley right in the eyes. 'Don't do that,' she said. 'If you want to be friends, don't do that.'

Riley nodded and turned her back again.

Harry had looked over at her. 'We're really bonding,' Holly mouthed, wiping spit off her hair. What Holly did not hear, as she went to clean herself up, was Riley blowing raspberries in her direction! The others didn't have the heart to tell her.

All the campers took turns preparing fruit and vegetable buckets for the animals, sometimes spending hours cutting and chopping. They were all getting a good insight into how to look after animals properly.

Now and then, Fionn would join them, to give them more information about the animals they were looking after, or just to keep an eye on them.

'Quitting time,' yawned Holly one day. 'I am so hungry and very tired from **talking to myself all day**!' she shouted, looking over her shoulder so Riley would hear. Riley just winked.

Fionn came over. 'Right, you lot,' he said. 'Great work again today. Let's go and have dinner. Any progress with Riley then, Holly?' he asked, as they headed towards camp.

'She likes me, I think,' Holly said without much confidence. 'I wish I could hug her. She seems like she could use a hug.'

'She'll let you hug her when she's ready, Holly. You're doing great work building her confidence and trust.'

Fionn was a lovely person. He was kind and fun, which Holly felt was the perfect mix for a camp leader. Harry reckoned that Fionn was dating Sinead, because he was always looking at her with that lovey-dovey smile that adults had!

At dinner, they were joined by Emme, her new friend Kate, the Barns boys and Ibby and Dibby. Like at most meals, poor Kate was interviewed as if she was on the *Late Show*. Tonight, Holly fired questions at her in between mouthfuls of chicken-licken legs and sweet-spud chippies, questions about her favourite colours, dolls, gymnastic ability ... it went on and on.

Kate answered the questions politely, even though her food was going cold. 'This is a nice family,' she thought. 'I'd love to have sisters ... but then again, they talk a lot!'

# *CHAPTER EIGHT*
## The Last Day

The Furry-baz wake-up horn blared as the Dixons were chatting in bed. They were so used to it now that they woke up naturally just before it.

'Last day,' said Emme, leaning on one elbow. 'I feel weird. I'm half excited to go home but half sad to leave here.'

'Me too,' Jess yawned. Like the others, she had made great friends at camp. They had all promised to write to each other when they went home.

'Hols,' Jess asked, 'are you okay?'

Holly was unusually quiet this morning. She had a pain in her tummy at the thought of not being with Riley every day. They had spoken to their parents at the weekend by using Uni, and her mum said that it was okay to feel sad.

'I'm okay, Jess,' Holly replied quietly, face down under the duvet. 'I just feel sad.'

'My sister has a massive heart,' Emme thought. Whatever Holly did when she was older, it would be a caring, kind job.

They all got dressed and ready for brekkie on their last day in camp.

'Porridgey-woridgey,' shouted Charlie the chef as the girls approached. He always made them smile, every single meal. This morning he was dressed up like a chicken. It was his costume for the last day, he explained. 'Last summer,' he said, pouring porridge into bowls, 'I dressed up as a salmon and I got stuck in the outfit for two days!'

No one knew what to say to that. A salmon was a very strange costume choice!

The group sat down for their last brekkie together. 'We are taking underwater photos today,' Emme and Kate were telling the others.

'Why, Emme?' asked Jess.

'Well, we've been cleaning the ocean bed for nearly four weeks. On day one, Oisín and his team of swimmers took underwater photos of what the ocean was like.'

They all nodded.

'So today, we're going to take photos of what it's like now! I'm so curious to see whether we have made a difference. They will be showing the photos at the Camp Circle before the disco later.'

The teams split up and headed to their zones for the last day.

Riley was waiting for Holly in her usual spot. As she approached, Riley whistled and smiled, turning around to show off her hair. As soon as Holly saw Riley, her mood lifted, and she felt happy. There was something about that crazy animal!

'Morning,' she said, as Harry headed off to the unicorns. 'I've been thinking about you a lot, you know,' Holly said, as she brushed the Chunga-Wunga's hair. 'I hope that you'll be okay when I go home. I'll be thinking about you the whole time.'

Holly's eyes began to fill up. 'I know you don't understand, but I want you to know that you are my **best friend**, and I will always love you, okay?'

Riley had been staring at her with a strange look on her face. Suddenly, Riley smiled to herself. Then she opened her arms wide and held them out to Holly for a hug. They hugged! They actually hugged, and Holly thought her heart would burst!

She very carefully separated from Riley. 'Thanks, pal,' she said. 'You've made my year.' Riley winked, and pretended to spit in her hair, for old times' sake.

As all this was going on, Jess and Hugo were checking the forest for any last bits of litter that might hurt the trees. The Treeps were sad the campers were leaving but were glad to have had their help.

By the beach, the ocean team were in their gear and in the water. For the last day, they were playing music on a radio on the beach, and it was great fun trying to dance and swim at the same time.

They gave the ocean bed another final sweep and found very little plastic. Even the turtles were gone – they were free now, so they could swim out to the deep sea.

'I'll miss this,' Emme said to Ollie Barns, as they floated peacefully, chilling after all their hard work was done.

'So will I,' Ollie said, ducking under the water to do a handstand. 'I'm defo coming back to Tír na nÓg next year, if our parents let us.'

'Definitely,' agreed Emme, thinking that it was nice that her annoying neighbour had become her friend. Now maybe they could hang out more at home.

Her new friend Kate lived far away, so she'd have to send a post-midge to drop off her letters.

After they had a final swim, they headed back to camp base to shower, have their dinner and get ready for the disco.

As they were approaching the Camp Circle, they could see Jess, Harry and Holly walking slowly down the path. Holly was crying and Emme immediately knew why.

'Come here, Hols,' she said, holding out her arms for a hug.

Holly came over and hugged her. 'My heart is broken,' she said, 'and I think Riley is sad too, because she wouldn't eat her dinner. She just disappeared.'

'Yeah, it was strange alright,' said Harry, joining the sisters. 'She actually disappeared, and we couldn't see her.'

'Holly, we'll ask Sir Prize if you can come back and see her someday,' said Jess, putting her hand on her big sister's back.

'It's not the same,' Holly wailed. She continued to sob so loudly that Oisín looked over, concerned.

Emme mouthed 'Riley' so that he would understand. All the other campers nodded too. Holly had done nothing but talk about 'my friend Riley' for four weeks.

The Dixon girls headed back to their caravan and got washed and dressed. Emme was wearing skinny jeans and a hoodie. Holly wore black leggings, a sparkly pink reversible T-shirt and her turquoise Converse. Jess wore her stripy onesie because, she said, it might get cold.

At dinner, there was a great air of excitement, as Sir Prize himself was calling in to personally hand out their certificates!

When they had finished off their final dessert, they sat at their tables and waited. Suddenly, there was a loud rumbling noise and the ground began to tremble.

'*Féach!*' said Sinead, standing up and pointing at the sky. A distant dot began to get bigger and bigger, and the campers gasped as it turned into a massive purple and turquoise dragon. Riding on its back was Sir Prize, looking handsome and smart in a red suit.

The dragon glided down and landed on top of the food station. Sir Prize slid off the dragon, somersaulting off the thatch roof and landing on his feet, like a circus performer. Everyone clapped and Emme could see that the camp leaders were so proud of their kind boss.

'*Comhghairdeas*, campers,' he said. 'I am so impressed with all of you and your hard work.

You have made such a difference, possibly more than you will ever know.' He smiled at them all and began to hand out certificates.

They were long pieces of heavy gold paper. Each had a name at the top, and a big red tick to show that the person had completed their work at the camp. They came in a poster roller case so they wouldn't rip.

After Sir Prize had presented the certs, he went over and high-fived Charlie. They had been fast friends for years.

'Now it's time to see some of your hard work,' said Oisín, standing beside a small projector.

He looked over at Sir Prize, who winked back and waved his fingers in the air. With that, the huge projector was lifted into the air and pictures filled the sky. It was such an amazing sight that everyone fell silent.

First, they looked at the ocean. On one side, there was dirty, murky water under a beautiful sky. Sea-green turtles were struggling to move, and plastic bottles and bags covered the seabed. On the other side, the sea was clear again, the sand was white and full of shells, and small fish swam in the water. It was amazing.

'**Woooow!**' said the entire camp at the same time.

Next, the projector showed some of the work that the campers had been doing with the animals, and Holly clapped when she saw herself and Harry on the screen.

The forest slides looked beautiful too, the tall trees stretching up to the sky like something from a movie. There were pictures of the Treeps too, and Jess cheered when her friend Emilette appeared.

After the final slide, Sir Prize started to clap, and the entire camp joined in. 'Now, let the *craic agus ceol* begin!' he said, as huge curtains fell down around the Camp Circle, turning it into a circus tent with the ceiling left open to the stars.

Chef Charlie's band took it away. A Treep joined him on an electric piano and Sir Prize himself stepped up to play the saxophone. Charlie was the main singer, and he belted out the songs as he played drums with his wooden spoons. He wasn't the *best* singer in the world … but he was happy!

They all danced the night away. Ollie Barns even asked Emme to dance, but she just blushed, made an excuse and ran away!

It was very dark by the time the music
ended. Sir Prize made his exit as exciting as his
entrance, waving at them all as he boarded the

dragon. 'Night everyone, *oíche mhaith*,' they all said to each other, heading to their caravans for one last night's sleep.

# CHAPTER NINE
## Back Home

'Wakey-wakey, you two,' said Emme to the lumps in the beds beside her. She was sad to be leaving, but also excited to see her parents and sleep in her own comfy bed.

She and Kate had planned to stay in touch. There were magical mirrors that they could organise in their schools. You could see and talk to anyone in the world, they were so clear. Emme just needed the right code to get to Kate's school.

'Morning,' said Holly, shooting up out of bed. She was desperate to say goodbye to Riley.

She was dressed, teeth brushed and ready in five minutes. Jess tried to copy her, but ended up tripping, banging her arm, and then crying, which delayed the process.

Off to brekkie they went to meet their friends at the Camp Circle. It sounded very noisy as they approached, with people clapping and laughing.

There was a real buzz in the camp. The sun was shining and it was a hot day. Charlie was juggling frying pans and they could smell sizzling saussie-wassies.

Charlie turned his music up quite high and began to show off his Irish dancing skills to an amused bunch of clapping campers. 'Come on, you lot, will you join in?' he said, as he saw the Dixons walking over.

'No way!' thought Emme, pretending to look around her, embarrassed.

But Jess flew over and was soon at the centre of the ring. She was finally getting to show off her dance routine!

Once Jess and Charlie had completed their dance, they bowed and everyone cheered. Then the saussie-wassie rollie buns were handed out and they all ate brekkie with gusto.

When the whistle blew, they cleaned up their plates and headed towards their group lines for the last time this summer.

'Are you okay, Hols?' Harry said, patting his friend on the back.

'Not really, Harry,' she said quietly. She had really felt responsibility for the first time in her life. She felt that she had to look after and protect Riley for ever. The thought of never seeing the Chunga-Wunga's face again made her want to cry.

'Look, chin up, Hols. Spend the morning with Riley,' he said, 'and don't waste time feeling sad.'

Holly, Jess and Harry headed off to the Animal Zone for the last time. Jess saw that Harriet and Sheila, the magical twin hens, were arguing. Harriet had her eyes closed as she was giving out, and Sheila was looking the other way. 'I'd love to know what they are fighting over,' thought Jess.

**'JESS! HARRY!'** Holly was yelling in a panic down by the gate. 'I can't find Riley anywhere, she's not in her house!' She was pacing now, really upset.

The three of them called Riley's name and waited to see if she was just far away in the back of her pen. She loved her food, so she should be here, waiting for her brekkie.

After a few minutes, Fionn came over. 'Riley's at the vet, guys,' he said. 'I totally forgot to tell you. Sorry. There's nothing to worry about,' he added, seeing the panicked looks on their faces, 'it's just a general check-up that she has every month.'

'I have to say goodbye to her, though,' said Holly, trying not to cry.

'I know, but you're not to worry. She's fine, and I'm sure that Sir Prize will let you come back to visit.'

Holly nodded, trying to be brave. She blew a kiss towards Riley's empty pen and walked away, thinking that she might as well go with Harry to say goodbye to the unicorns.

Jess joined them after helping Harriet and Sheila make up – it turned out the hens had been fighting about an old boyfriend.

Before they knew it, it was midday and time to go home. All the campers headed back to base to collect their things and head back to the outside world.

With their backpacks on their shoulders, they all hugged and said goodbye. The sisters said 'See you later' jokingly to the Barns boys, as they were neighbours. Emme and Kate made a pinkie promise to stay friends for ever. Ibby and Dibby high-fived the Barns boys.

The gang went up the pathway behind Sinead, waving goodbye to Charlie as they left. It was strange to think that they had been here for four weeks – it felt like only a weekend had gone by.

Standing behind the door were Mr and Mrs Dixon, Mr and Mrs Barns and Sir Prize.

'Welcome back, boys,' said Mr Barns, whispering as usual.

They hugged their parents and thanked Sinead and Sir Prize for an amazing time.

'I hear that you all worked very hard,' Sir Prize said to the fairies. They nodded.

'Well, remember,' said Sir Prize with a wink, 'good things happen to good people. Safe home.' And he walked back into the castle.

Outside, there was a Butterfly Taxi waiting for them. 'My babies are back,' said Mrs Dixon,

kissing them all and hugging them tightly. 'I'm
so glad you enjoyed your time at Tír na nÓg.'

On the way hom

stories about the camp

Dixon noticed that Hol

'Need to talk, love?' she

to her parents about Rile

'You'll see her again, I

dad, opening the front door. Why don't you all

go up to your room and dump your backpacks?'

'Okay,' the girls said, feeling exhausted after

their long day.

Nothing prepared them for what happened

next.

Holly opened the door, and sitting on her

bed was … **Riley**! For the first time in her life,

Holly was speechless.

'Well, girls,' said Mrs Dixon, coming in with

their dad. 'We have been talking about getting a

me. We spoke to Sir Prize and he

that the three of you had learned how to

responsible. He trusts you to take care of her.'

'When Fionn said she was at the vet, he meant her new home here,' their dad laughed. 'We've built a special den for Riley down the road as she needs her own space, but she will spend time here too.'

'Now she's a Dixon!' Holly said running over and hugging Riley, before the Chunga-Wunga turned around to have her hair brushed. 'Thank you so much, Mum and Dad!'

Their dad cleared his throat. 'So I hope this means that you won't be using Farmer George as a dartboard ever again.'

The sisters nodded so fast their heads nearly fell off.

That night, when Riley had settled in her new pen, the family had dinner together and got into their pyjamas. Over hot chocolate in the kitchen, feeling happy and cosy, Emme asked, 'So, family, what is our next adventure?'

Mrs Dixon looked at Mr Dixon and said, 'Girls, umm … how do you feel about boats?'